For Craig and Wesley, who
are my home; and for my
parents, exiled from theirs
— L.H.

To my mom and my brother
for the many airplane
flights taken to visit and
support me
— S.P.

Tundra Books, an imprint of Tundra Book Group, a division of Penguin Random House of
Canada Limited

Library and Archives Canada Cataloguing in Publication

Title: On this airplane / Lourdes Heuer ; illustrated by Sara Palacios.
Names: Heuer, Lourdes, author. | Palacios, Sara, illustrator.
Identifiers: Canadiana (print) 20210293160 | Canadiana (ebook) 20210293187 |
ISBN 9780735268609 (hardcover) | ISBN 9780735268616 (EPUB)
Classification: LCC PZ7.1.H48 On 2022 | DDC j813/.6—dc23

Published simultaneously in the United States of America by Tundra Books of Northern
New York, an imprint of Tundra Book Group, a division of Penguin Random House of
Canada Limited

Library of Congress Control Number: 2021944910

Edited by Samantha Swenson
Designed by Jennifer Griffiths
The illustrations were created with gouache, cut paper and digital media.
The text was set in Founders Grotesk Text.

Printed in China

www.penguinrandomhouse.ca

1 2 3 4 5   26 25 24 23 22

Penguin
Random House
TUNDRA BOOKS

On This Airplane

Words by
Lourdes Heuer

Illustrations by
Sara Palacios

tundra

On this airplane, there is
a pilot living her dream,

one passenger daydreaming
and another fast asleep.

On this airplane, there is someone doing important work and someone in the service of work that is important.

On this airplane,
someone travels solo,
two travel as one,
three return
and four set out.

The cabin hums.
Air vents whoosh.
Left engines rumble,
right engines roar
before . . .

. . . takeoff!

On this airplane,
ice cubes melt.
Ice crystals bloom.

On this airplane,
a bookworm reads a textbook.

A baby reads a face.

On this airplane,
a seat reclines waaaay back.
A tray drops herky-jerky.

There is turbulence!
Up, down. Up, down.
Drinks drip drop.
Tummies flip flop . . .

. . . but here is a hand to hold and there is a helping hand.

On this airplane,
someone lends an earbud.
Someone lends an ear.
Someone makes a fuss . . .

someone makes a friend.

On this airplane,
a sleepyhead awakens,
a daydreamer still daydreams

and a pilot touches down.

On this airplane,
the passengers line up
to reach the door,
to cross the bridge,
to pass the gate . . .

. . . that leads . . .